A Place to Sleep

by Holly Meade

Marshall Cavendish • New York

Library of Congress Cataloging-in-Publication Data
Meade, Holly.
A place to sleep / Holly Meade.
p. cm.
Summary: Presents a variety of animals and the places where they
might sleep, from a bear snoozing in the arms of a tree to a boy in bed.
ISBN 0-7614-5096-3
1. Animals--Juvenile fiction. [1. Animals--Fiction.
2. Sleep--Fiction. 3. Bedtime--Fiction. 4. Stories in rhyme.] I. Title.
PZ10.3.M46 Pl 2001   [E]--dc21   00-052368

The text of this book is set in 22 point Leawood.
The illustrations are collages.
Printed in Hong Kong
First edition

6 5 4 3 2 1

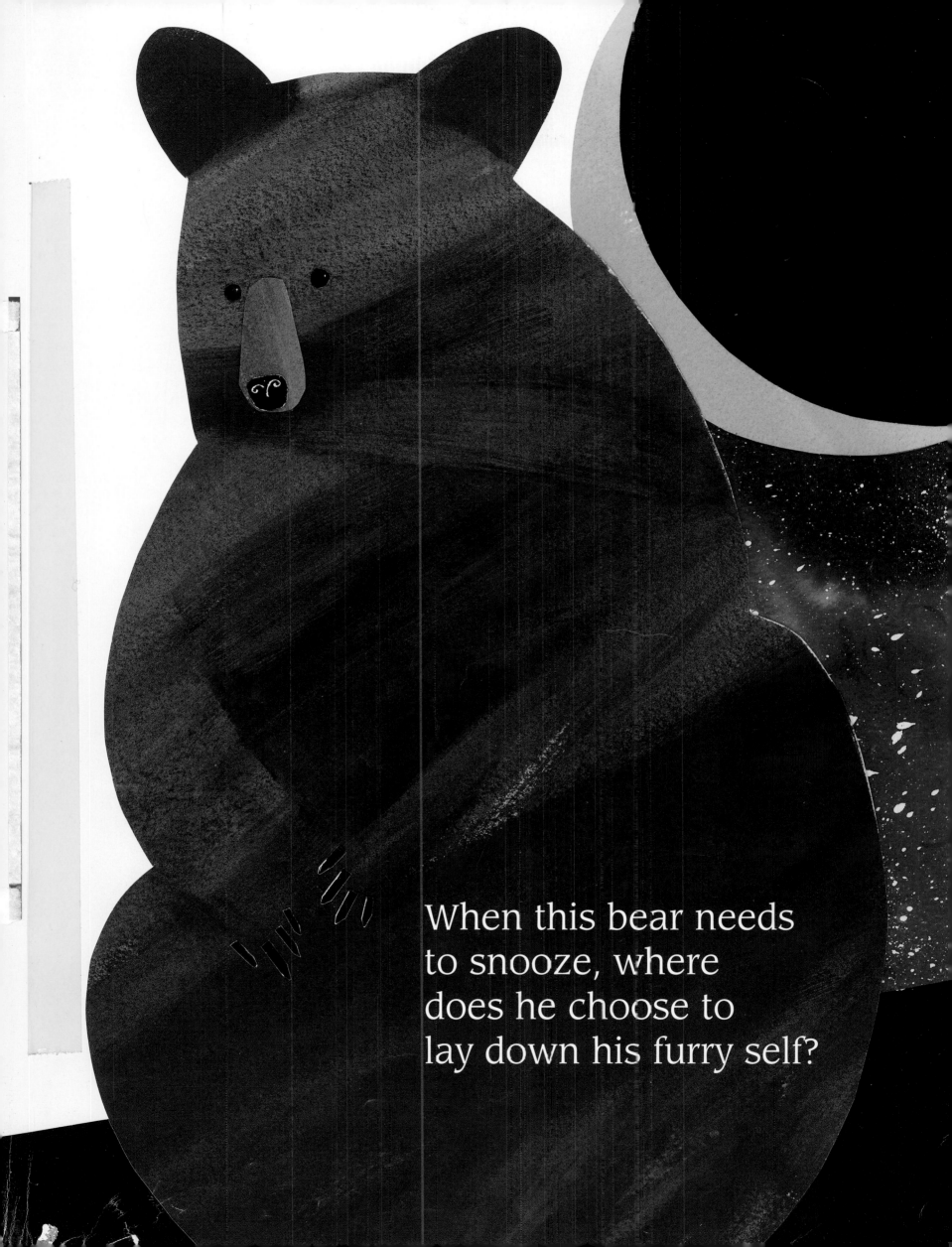

When this bear needs
to snooze, where
does he choose to
lay down his furry self?

In the arms of a
tree is a good place
for a slumbering
bear to slump.

Where might this sleek seal sleep at the

end of an underwater day?

On a lone sand beach,
her head on a stone,
is a fine place to
dream for a seal.

And for this handsome cat

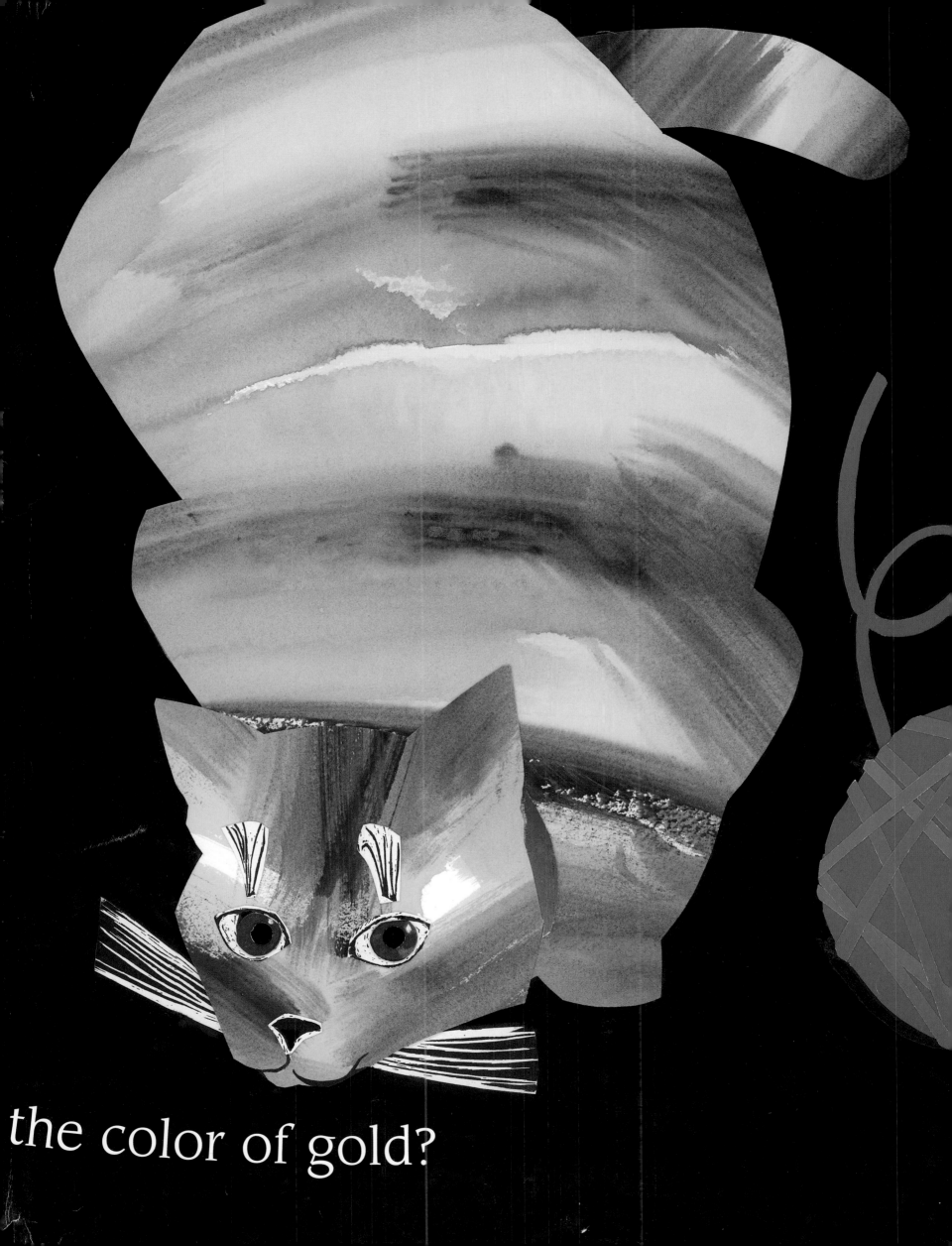

the color of gold?

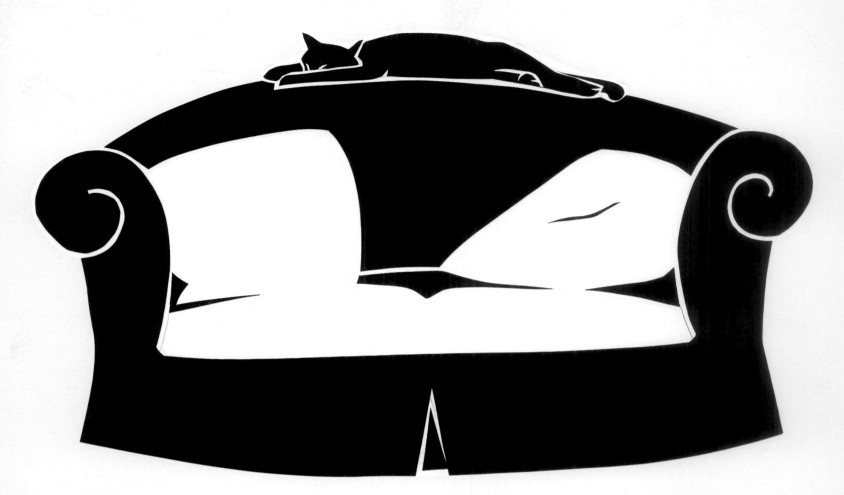

Aaahhh . . . over
the couchback with a
s t r e t c h and a
p u r r r r r r is the
perfect place for him.

This minuscule

mouse needs a nest to rest in.

She certainly does.
A very small and
very secret place is the
wish of every mouse.

When this elephant needs to snooze,

where does he choose to rest his

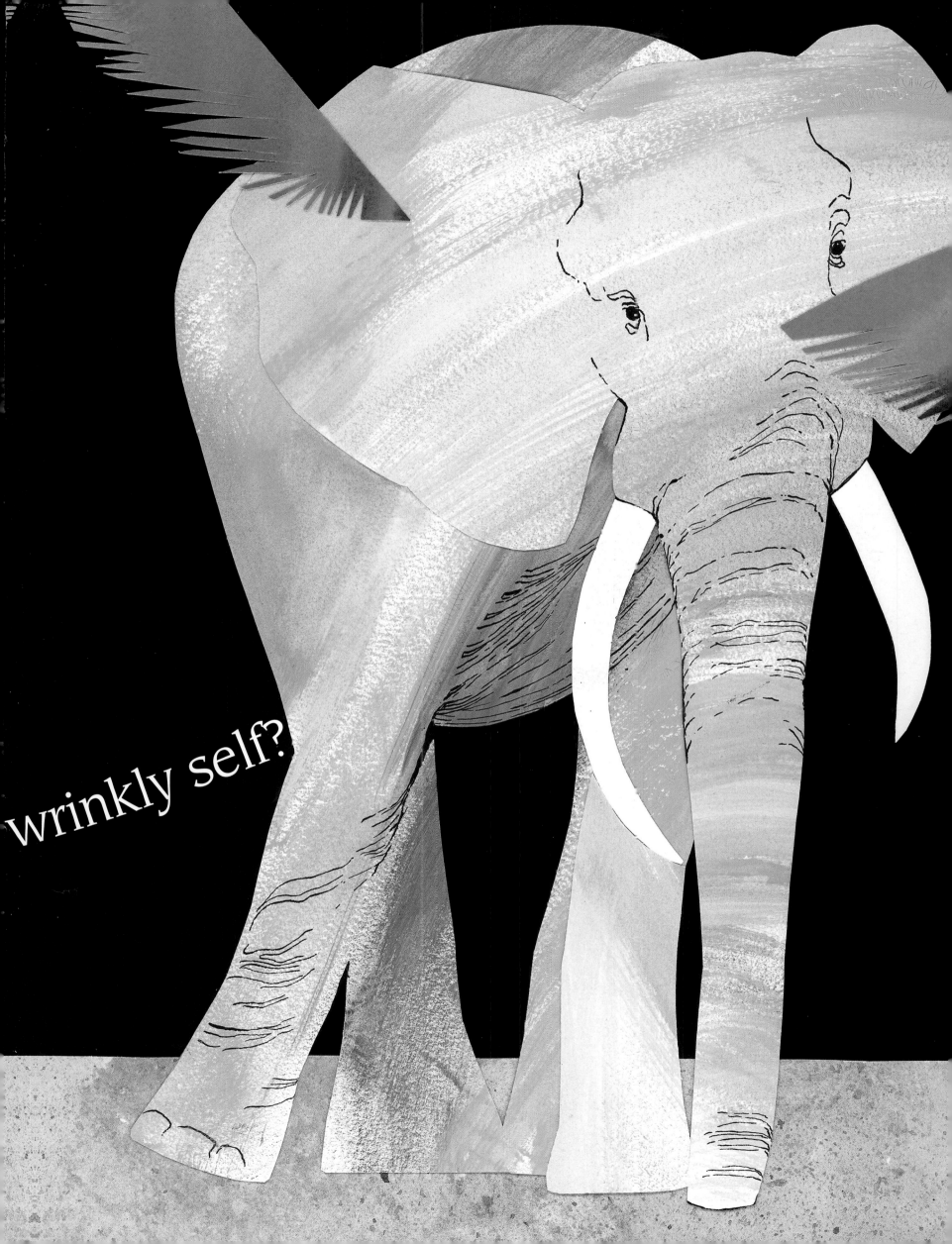

wrinkly self?

Hard to believe, but!
Standing on his
feet he nods and
naps as necessary.

This oh so heavy hippo gets weary

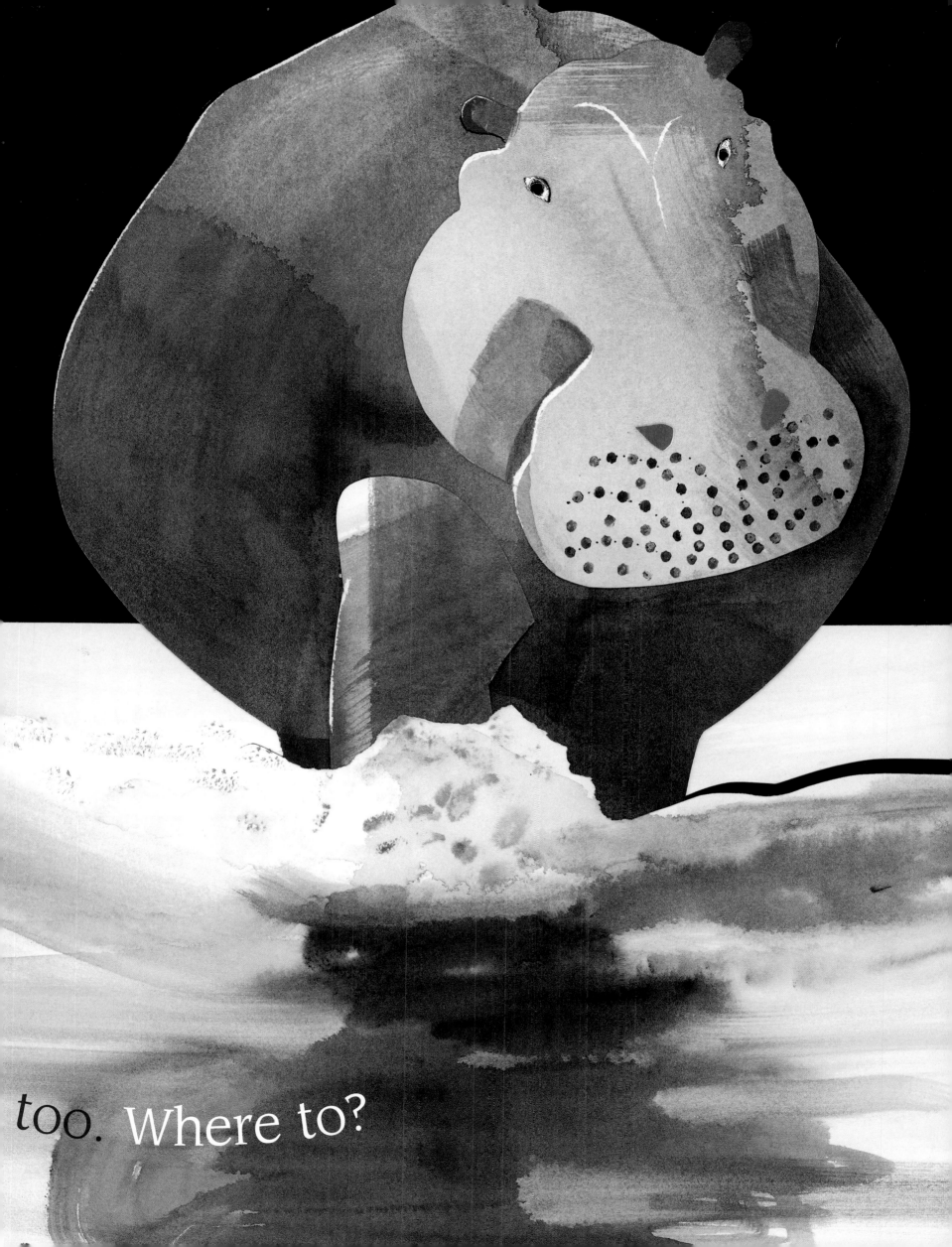

too. Where to?

Mud, thick and
soft, will hold his
hulk in comfort.

In what place does this puppy find

If she dares she'll take the living room chair. The one place she's not allowed!

When his bananas are all gone, and sleep is coming on, where might

High to a limb,
and limp as a peel,
that's the place
you'll find him.

And this fast jack-rabbit,
ears all a-flap, where does she hop to

in hopes of a rest?

To her cozy burrow
she bounds, a
warm dark pocket
below the earth.

Where oh where
would this fish float to, to find

a siesta of sorts?

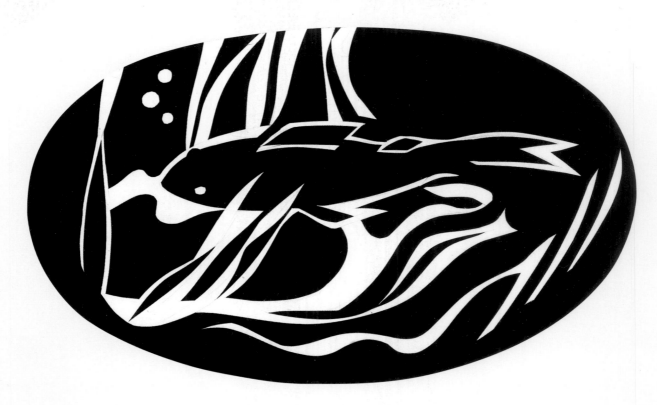

The shadows of the
shallows suit this fish.
Hard to believe, but!
He sleeps with his
eyes wide open.

When this duck's feeling drowsy, in

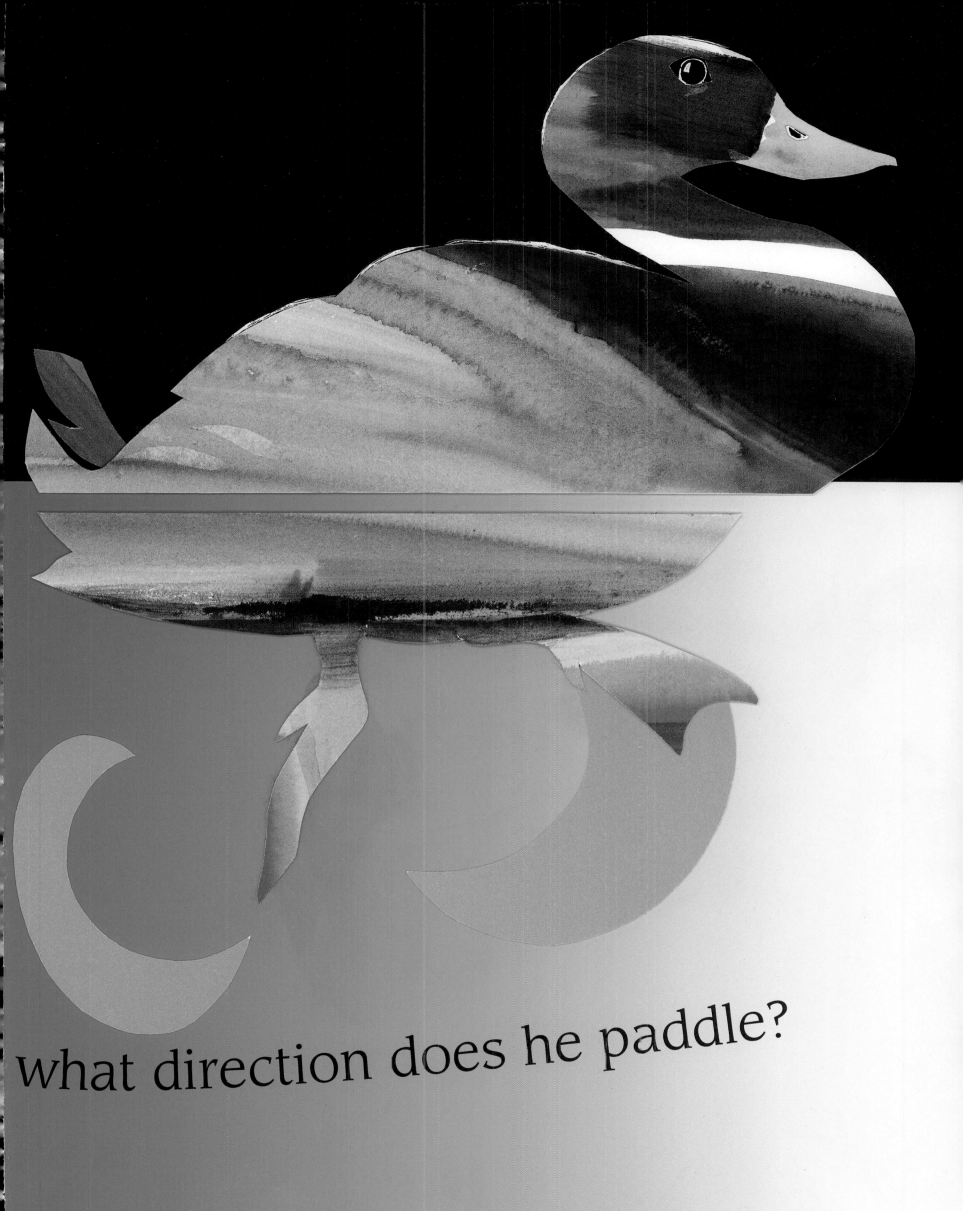

what direction does he paddle?

He pumps his weary duck feet
toward the safety of the duck house,
with his family close behind.

And what
about
these two?

When this girl
needs to snooze,
where does
SHE choose?

When this boy is getting sleepy, where does HE slumber? Where do they go?

To beds clean and soft,
under covers and with kisses,

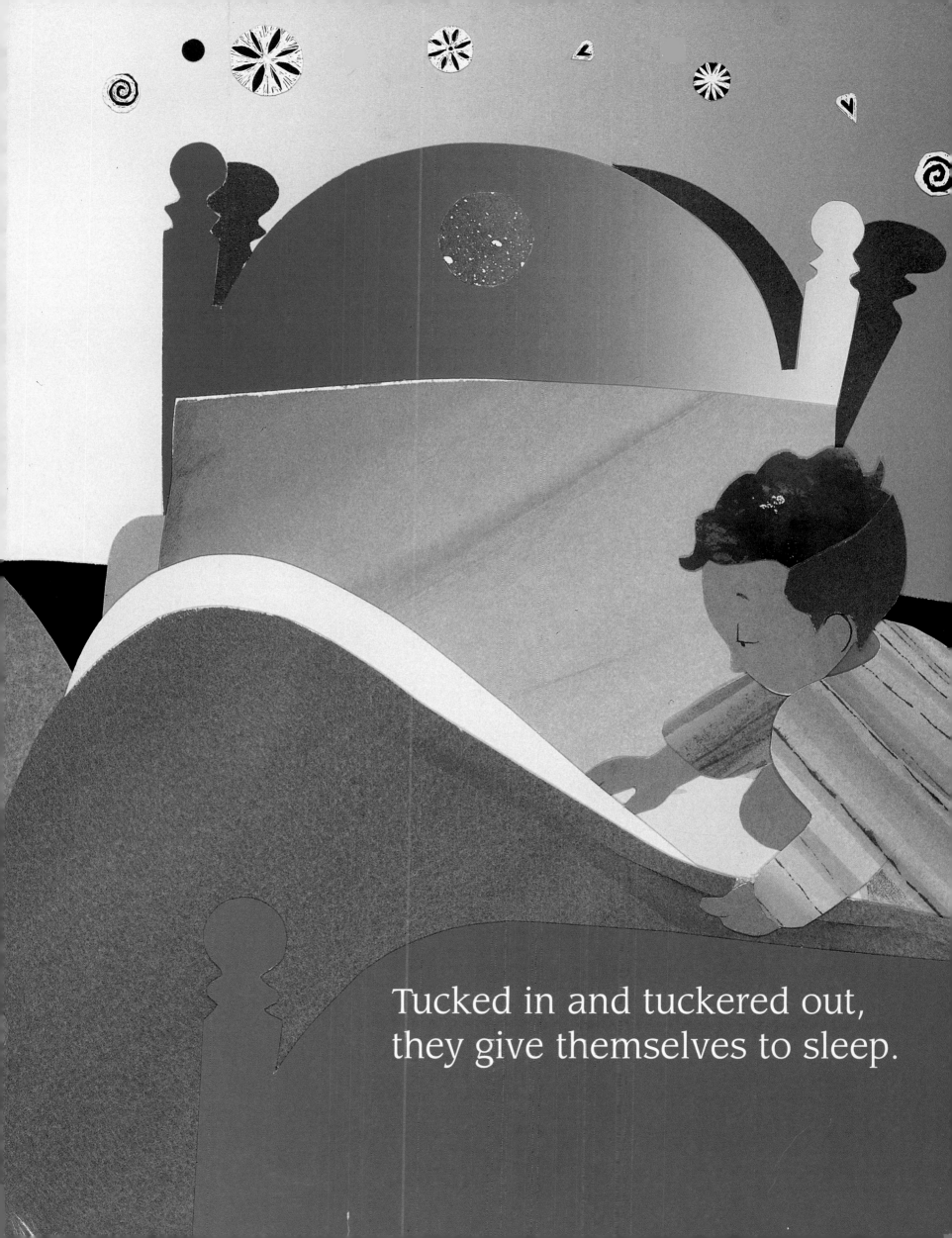

Tucked in and tuckered out,
they give themselves to sleep.

They sink, sink down in warmth,

while their dreams rise and rise.

In their very own beds, where they choose to snooze. Good night.